Written by Valerie Hall. Text ©1990 Valerie Hall.

Illustrated by Pam Storey.

This edition published exclusively for Bookmart Limited.
by
Grandreams Limited
Jadwin House, 205/211 Kentish Town Road, London, NW5 2JU.

Printed in Czech Republic.

MY BUMPER
BOB~A~LONG BUNNIES
◄— STORYBOOK —►

This Book Belongs To:

....

....

....

Age: ....

CONTENTS

A Day At The Fair

Barty's Big Adventure

The BOB~A~LONG BUNNIES
◄— HOUSE HUNTING —►

The Bob-a-Long family
had settled down for a quiet evening in their cosy
burrow. Mr. Bob-a-Long, tired from a hard day
spent foraging for food, was snoozing. Mrs. Bob-a-
Long was tucking the twins, Buffy and Bonnie, into
their cot. Barty Bob-a-Long was gazing into space,
dreaming, and his sister, Blossom, was sorting
through some coloured stones she had found and
thought would make a pretty necklace.

"Pass me that cot cover, please, Barty," said Mrs. Bob-a-Long to her son. Barty blinked at her, not understanding. He was far away in a fairy land rescuing a tiny pixie from a wicked wizard. His mother pointed to a curly, sheep's wool blanket close to his feet. Still dreaming, he took it over to his mother not noticing the stool in the middle of the room which he somersaulted over landing with the blanket over his head. Buffy and Bonnie giggled and Barty looked anxiously to see if his father had woken up.

Mr. Bob-a-Long glared at his son. Then his nose twitched and he began to laugh. "You really are the clumsiest bunny ever to have been born," he chuckled.

"Well, we know where he gets that from," commented his wife. "Your great uncle Bartlemy. He's taken on his clumsy ways as well as his name," she added, taking the blanket off Barty's head and laying it over the twins, who were still giggling. "Now they'll never get to sleep."

"And what about my stones?" said Blossom. "Barty knocked them all over the place, I'll never be able to find them." So Barty offered to help pick them up.

As Barty picked up the stones he pretended they were magic and would grant him any wish he cared to make. He held them tightly in his hand and wished hard. It was the same wish that he always made, that he could meet an elf who would become his friend and take him on magical adventures. He once told Blossom about his wish but she had only laughed at him and said, "surely you don't still believe in fairies?" After that, Barty kept his wishes to himself for he did believe in fairies - and elves and goblins and he spent most of his time dreaming about them.

The next day,
Mr. Bob-a-Long set off
as usual to look for food
for his family.
Everything was peaceful
inside the little burrow.
Mrs. Bob-a-Long was
playing with the twins,
Barty was imagining
that a pixie was
teaching him to fly and
Blossom was stringing
together her coloured
stones. Suddenly
they heard heavy
footsteps outside. The
bunnies looked towards
the entrance of the
burrow and saw a pair
of boots go clumping
by followed by four
brown and white paws.
The paws stopped and
turned and the next
thing the bunnies
knew a dog's nose was
sniffing its way into their
home.

"Go away," Mrs. Bob-a-Long shouted at the dog. "Go away at once." But the dog took no notice. It was too busy scratching its way into the burrow. The twins took fright and started to cry.

"What are we going to do?" wailed Mrs. Bob-a-Long. "Barty! Do something, quickly."

While Barty stood thinking how useful it would be to know a spell that would make dogs disappear, Blossom began throwing her coloured stones at the animal, one by one. They were very hard and must have hurt because it gave a sudden yelp and backed off. The bunnies kept quiet and still until they were certain that it would not return.

When Mr. Bob-a-Long got home his wife told him all that had happened that day.

"This field isn't a safe place to live in anymore," she cried. "It is time that we moved away."

Her husband thought for a while and then nodded his head. "Very well, tomorrow I shall go to the big forest and look for a new burrow. We should be safer living there."
"And I'm coming with you," said Blossom, eagerly.

Her mother pointed out that as Barty was the eldest it was only right and proper that he should accompany his father on such a trip.

"Oh, he won't be any use," scoffed Blossom, "he'd be too busy day-dreaming to remember what he was looking for."

"Well, Barty, do you want to come?" his father asked. Barty just shrugged and turned away. He was feeling pretty miserable. Perhaps Blossom was right and he wasn't any use, after all, he'd made a rotten job of defending the burrow that afternoon. Then he had an idea.

"I'll show them," he thought. "I'll go out tomorrow and find a new burrow myself. The biggest, warmest, safest burrow in Bunnydom. And it won't be in some dark and gloomy forest. No. It'll be in some jolly place, like a river. There might even be water sprites living there who would show me their underwater home." Once again, Barty's imagination was getting the better of him.

Early next morning, after Mr. Bob-a-Long and Blossom had left for the big forest, Barty slipped out of the burrow as quietly as he could, bumping into the table and knocking over the hat stand as he went. Once outside he bobbed off across the field towards the river and soon arrived at a part that flowed past some rushes.

A clump of yellow marsh marigolds were growing nearby and Barty thought how much Blossom would enjoy picking them.

A frog suddenly croaked at him from behind the rushes and Barty was sure it had said, "welcome."

"What a friendly place this is," Barty thought.

Just then a water
vole scurried up.

"What do you
want?" it said, rather
snappily.

"I'm looking for a
home," said Barty.

"Well, you're not
having mine," said the
vole.

Barty explained
that he didn't want the
vole's home as he was
sure it wouldn't be big
enough. "You see, I have
a mother and father, a
brother and two sisters."

"We don't want any more living round here. There's not enough to go round as it is," grumbled the vole.

"Not enough what?" asked Barty.

"Not enough anything," answered the little creature, mysteriously, as it went on gathering moss for his home. Barty was dying to ask one more question. "Er ... are there any water sprites living hereabouts?"

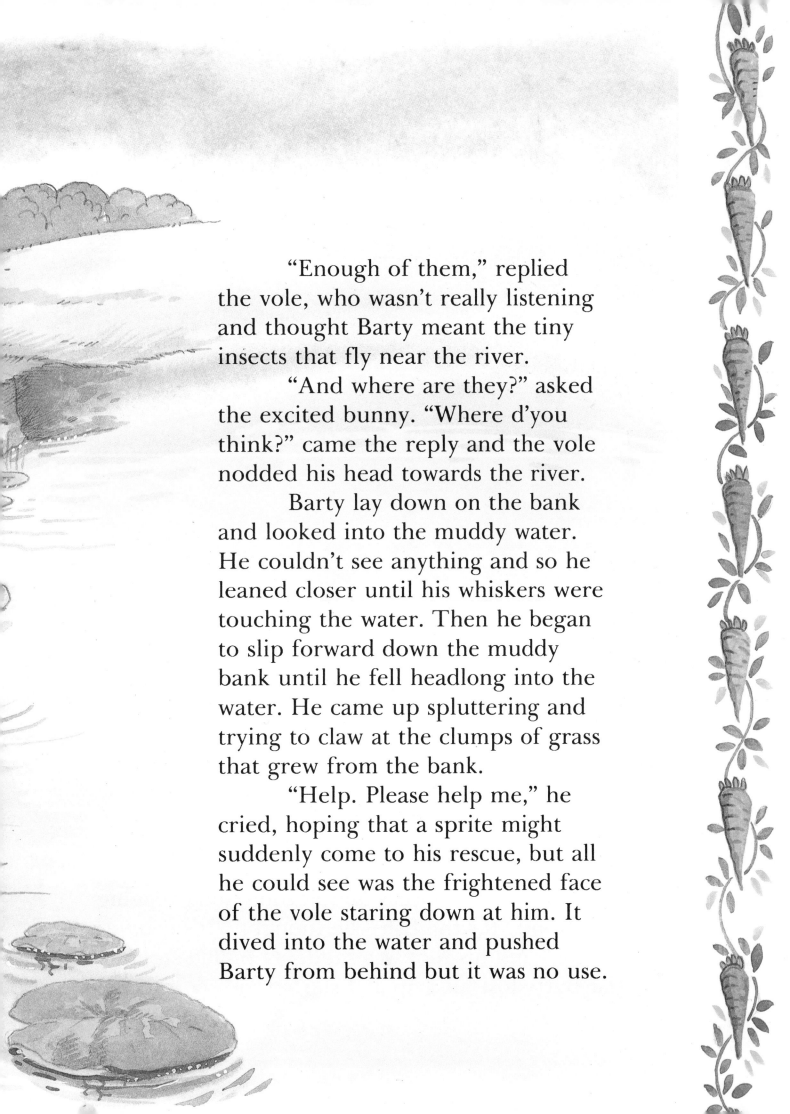

"Enough of them," replied the vole, who wasn't really listening and thought Barty meant the tiny insects that fly near the river.

"And where are they?" asked the excited bunny. "Where d'you think?" came the reply and the vole nodded his head towards the river.

Barty lay down on the bank and looked into the muddy water. He couldn't see anything and so he leaned closer until his whiskers were touching the water. Then he began to slip forward down the muddy bank until he fell headlong into the water. He came up spluttering and trying to claw at the clumps of grass that grew from the bank.

"Help. Please help me," he cried, hoping that a sprite might suddenly come to his rescue, but all he could see was the frightened face of the vole staring down at him. It dived into the water and pushed Barty from behind but it was no use.

"Enough is enough," panted the vole. "I'm going for help," and off he ran.

Poor Barty was terrified. He'd heard that a big fish lived in this river, an enormous pike that ate little creatures for its tea. His bunny heart went thump-thump-thump as he felt something tugging at his foot. "It's the fish," he thought. "It's come to get me," and his foot was suddenly pulled so hard that Barty lost his grip and started to sink into the water. Then something else pulled at his ears and he found himself being lifted onto dry land with a long piece of river weed wrapped around his foot.

"Oh, Barty," a voice said, "what have you been up to?"

Standing there were Mr. Bob-a-Long, Blossom and the vole.

Their home hunting finished, Mr. Bob-a-Long and Blossom had arrived at the burrow only to

find that Barty was missing. They were on their way to the river to look for him when they had bumped into the vole. Mr. Bob-a-Long kept thanking him for helping to rescue his son, which embarrassed the vole as it was partly his fault that Barty had fallen in.

"There are lots of flowers there for me to pick," joined in Blossom.

"And there are no rivers for you to fall in," they said together.

That night, when Barty was dropping off to sleep, he began to think that maybe a forest wouldn't be such a bad place to live in after all. Forests could sometimes be magic places and there might be a wood nymph or a pixie living there.

"And who knows ....." yawned Barty, "there might even be an elf."

The BOB~A~LONG BUNNIES
◄ MOVING DAY ►

The Bob-a-Long family
were leaving their burrow on the edge of the
cornfield and moving to a new home under the old
oak tree in the middle of the big forest. Their
furniture was packed onto half of a hollowed out log
with grass twine tied to it so that it could be pulled
along like a sledge. In the other half the twins,
Buffy and Bonnie, were tucked
in and ready to go.

Blossom was wearing all her belongings. She had on both of her straw hats and all her necklaces of dried flowers. Barty carried nothing but an old stick he had found that was such a peculiar twisted shape that he was sure it must be magic. It hung from around his neck on a piece of twine.

When everyone was ready the Bob-a-Longs took a last look at their old home.

"We've had some happy times here," sighed Mr. Bob-a-Long.

"And some worrying ones," added Mrs. Bob-a-Long, thinking of the day that a dog tried to dig its way into their home. Then she gave the floor a last flick over with her twig broom so that it might be clean and neat for the next occupants, packed the broom with the rest of the things and left with her family.

The Bob-a-Longs set off across the field towards the big forest. Mr. Bob-a-Long pulled the log full of furniture and Barty pulled the log

carrying his brother and sister. But, as usual, Barty drifted off into a dream world and didn't notice the mole hills along the way. Every time the log bumped over one the twins flew into the air. They thought it great fun until Bonnie fell out, bumped her nose and started to cry.

"Really, Barty, can you do nothing properly?" scolded Mrs. Bob-a-Long. "You'd better pull the furniture, at least you can't hurt that."

But Barty made an even worse job of pulling the furniture. He would forget to look where he was going, pull the log over a bump and a chair or a table would fall off. In the end, Blossom was made to follow Barty and pick up anything he dropped.

"Now we must

stick close to each other," Mr. Bob-a-Long told his family as they entered the big forest. "The path winds about and it is very easy to get lost."

"Listen to what your father is saying, Barty," said Mrs. Bob-a-Long. "We want to arrive at our new home together - furniture and all!"

For a while the bunnies stayed close together until Barty started lagging behind and Blossom dashed on ahead to pick some bluebells. Mrs. Bob-a-Long was too busy comforting Buffy, who was crying because the forest was dark and scary, to notice them.

Barty was dreaming again. For him the forest was a magical place and he gazed about hoping to find a fairy or a pixie behind one of the trees. A sudden noise broke his dream and he turned to find the hat stand had fallen off the log and a trail of cups and bowls stretching through the forest.

"Bother," he muttered, and went back to pick them all up.

When Barty had put everything on to the log he looked around for his family, but no one was in sight.

"Now Barty, there's no need to be afraid," he told himself. "I'll just follow the path and I'll soon catch up with the others." And with that comforting thought he set off. But the path quickly disappeared round a tree and when it reappeared it had divided in two and Barty didn't know which to choose. He started to feel a little bit frightened.

Then Barty had
an idea. He remembered
the funny old stick he
had brought with him
and, convinced that it was
magic, felt sure that it
could somehow show him
the way.

"I'll throw it in the
air," he thought, "and
whichever way it points
when it lands that will be
the way to go." So he
held the stick in his paw,
closed his eyes then threw
it high into the air over
his head.

There was a
clunk, a yell, a rustling,

like something falling through the branches of a tree, and a thud. Barty was almost too scared to open his eyes, but when he did he saw on the ground before him, rubbing his chin and looking very cross indeed, a little man dressed in a suit of leaves. Barty felt shivers of excitement run from the tips of his ears to the end of his tail for he knew that his dream had come true and he was actually in the presence of a real, live elf.

Barty was so thrilled that he couldn't speak. He simply watched as the elf got up, dusted himself down, flexed his arms and legs to see if any bones were broken and then started to walk away. This was not the way Barty had pictured his first meeting with an elf. In his dreams he imagined that they would talk together, become friends and go off on adventures. Well, the elf was certainly going off somewhere, but on his own and Barty had to do something to stop him.

He suddenly found his voice. "Don't go!" he cried.

The elf turned and glared at the bunny. "Give me one good reason why I should stay."

"I... I... I've always wanted to meet an elf," Barty told him.

"Have you indeed. And I suppose that knocking me out of that tree was your way of saying 'hello'."

"Oh no," said Barty. "I didn't even know you were there. I really am very sorry, but I was trying to find the way home with my magic stick." The elf roared with laughter. "Magic, that old twig? What a stupid bunny you are."

Barty was glad that the subject of magic had come up and although he was a little frightened of the elf he was determined to ask him a particular question.

"Can you do magic?" Barty asked.

"Of course I can," snapped the elf.

"Then could you magic me to the old oak tree in the middle of the forest?" Barty thought that magic was the only thing that would get him home.

The elf became angry and went quite red in the face. "You hit me on the chin, knock me out of a tree, nearly break all my bones and then expect me to perform magic for you, why you're even more stupid than I thought."

He started to walk off in a huff, but the pile of furniture caught his eye and he stopped. "What's all this?" he asked, "firewood?" Barty told him what it was and explained about moving to a new home and getting separated from his family and that now he was completely lost. All the time the elf rummaged through the furniture, picking up a chair or a bowl and looking at it. He finally held up the hat stand and said, "I like this. If you give it to me I will do some magic for you, but I must warn you that magic is not always what you expect it to be."

Barty was in a dilemma. If he went home without the hat stand he would probably get into trouble, but if he didn't give the hat stand to the elf he might never get home at all.

"All right, you can have it," he said, at last. "But before you do your magic will you please tell me your name."

"It is Edwin," said the elf, proudly.

"That's a very good name for an elf," said Barty. "Mine's Barty Bob-a-Long."

"And that's a very stupid name, even for a bunny," grinned Edwin. "Now shut your eyes tight and remember, Barty Bob-a-Long, magic isn't always what you expect it to be." Then Edwin spun Barty around and around until the little bunny began to feel quite dizzy.

When the spinning stopped Barty opened his eyes. The elf had disappeared and Barty was in exactly the same spot as before. Now it was his turn to get angry. He shook a paw in the air and shouted so

loud that his voice echoed
through the forest, "give
me back our hat stand!"
But neither the elf nor
the hat stand appeared.

Through a blur of tears Barty saw a bluebell lying on a path just ahead of him. Near it was another bluebell and further on, another. Barty gasped. "It's a bluebell trail to lead me to home. Thank you, Edwin," he called, as he scampered off. A very short while later the bluebells led him into a sunny clearing in the middle of which stood a gnarled, old oak tree.

His family were so happy to see Barty again, although his father was a bit cross with Barty for leaving the furniture behind as Mr. Bob-a-Long had to go back into the forest to fetch it. When he returned he was scratching an ear and looking rather puzzled. "It's most odd," he said. "Everything's here except the hat stand and I can't find that anywhere."

Barty was about to tell his family all about meeting Edwin when Blossom interrupted.

"Aren't you going to thank me for getting you out of the forest?" Barty didn't know what his sister was talking about.

"As soon as we noticed that you weren't with us, I thought of laying a trail of bluebells to help you find your way," she bragged.

Poor Barty's head was filled with
confusing thoughts as he lay there in his strange,
new home unable to get to sleep that night. He
remembered the elf's words to him, "Magic isn't
always what you expect it to be," and he wondered if
Edwin really could do magic? And would he ever see
him again? And what in Bunnydom
did an elf want with
a hat stand?

The BOB~A~LONG BUNNIES
AT OAK TREE SCHOOL

The Bob-a-Long Bunnies' new home was much larger than their old one. There was a large burrow, like a sitting room, and off it ran several tunnels leading to smaller burrows, which were the bedrooms. Barty and Blossom each had their own burrow and Blossom had hung her straw hats and necklaces on the tree roots that poked through the walls. Barty hadn't anything in his, apart from his bed, but he planned to fill it later with magical things.

The morning after the bunnies moved into their new home Blossom and Barty asked if they could go outside to explore. Mrs. Bob-a-Long was busy spring-cleaning and glad to get them out from under her feet.

"Don't forget that your father said you were not to go into the forest, not until you know the paths better," she reminded them. Barty and Blossom nodded and hurried along the tunnel that led to a hole in the ground above, where they popped out their heads.

Although the old oak was deep in the heart of the forest, the other trees had stopped growing a little way away from it to form a lovely, sunny clearing where flowers grew and a brook burbled away happily.

"Don't fall in," teased Blossom, reminding Barty of the time he fell into the river near his old home. To show that he wasn't afraid, he hopped over to the brook, tripped on a stone and just saved himself from another wetting. He lay on his stomach listening to his sister's giggles until they faded away and he knew she had gone off to explore on her own.

Barty was glad to be alone. He wanted some time to himself to think about Edwin, the elf he had met in the forest the day before, and how he was going to find him again. But the sun was warm and Barty felt so comfortable that his eyes began to close and thinking became dreaming.

He dreamed that he was in the forest and that Edwin kept popping out from behind bushes and trees and disappearing again. When Barty awoke he knew he just had to go back into the forest to look for the elf and so, forgetting his father's words, he jumped up and headed for the trees.

At first he didn't venture too far into the forest as he was afraid of getting lost, but when he could find no sign of the elf he had no choice but to go a little further.

"Edwin," he called. "Edwin, it's me, Barty Bob-a-Long. If you're there, won't you please answer?"

"What are you doing here?" said a voice that made Barty almost jump right out of his skin. He swung round, hoping to see the elf but found himself looking into the angry face of his father. Barty was in serious trouble.

Back home, his ears hanging down in shame, Barty listened as his father told him off for disobeying instructions. By the time Mr. Bob-a-Long had finished with him he was beginning to think that he never wanted to see an elf again as long as he lived.

"The reason I came looking for you," said Mr. Bob-a-Long, not sounding quite so cross, "was to tell you that I had some news for you and Blossom. This morning I enrolled the two of you at Professor Bounder's Oak Tree School. You start tomorrow."

Next day, with well brushed fur and nice clean

whiskers, Blossom and Barty were ready for their day at school. Mrs. Bob-a-Long gave them their lunch, wrapped in a large dock leaf, and sent them scrambling up the tunnel into the sunlight.

Professor Bounder's classes were held on the other side of the oak tree's enormous trunk and when Barty and Blossom arrived several bunnies, some squirrels and couple of wood mice were there already. They stopped talking and playing pat-a-paw to watch the two Bob-a-Longs shyly take their places and to snigger at Barty falling over a wood mouse. But the next minute everyone was quiet and sitting up straight; for Professor Bounder had arrived.

He was a stern looking bunny with greying fur and he carried a stick which he used to point at the pupils when he wanted them to answer a question or tap them on the ears when they weren't paying attention. Barty and Blossom spent the morning learning to count up to five, at least Blossom did; Barty only got as far as two and then his thoughts wandered and he had his ears tapped by Professor Bounder.

At break time Blossom made friends with a girl bunny called Flora Furrypaws who knew where to find the best flowers for trimming hats and making necklaces. Barty kept to himself. He didn't much like school and couldn't have cared less how many carrots made five. All Barty wanted to learn about was fairies and wizards and magic.

After break Barty had his ears tapped twice more for dozing during class and was about to nod off again when something hitting him on the head made him look up. What he saw made his eyes open wide, for sitting on a branch grinning down at him was Edwin the elf. Barty watched as the troublesome creature tossed another acorn at the Professor. He swung round and glared at Barty.

"Was that you, Bob-a-Long?" he asked, rubbing his neck.

"No sir," said Barty, his innocent eyes ready to brim over with tears. Although strict, Professor Bounder had a soft heart and in all his years of teaching he had never made a pupil cry.

"Very well then," he muttered, doubtfully, "but... er... see that it doesn't happen again," and he hastily returned to the lesson.

The afternoon was to be spent on a nature walk and, true to his name, the Professor bounded through the forest with his class sometimes struggling to keep up.

"Don't dawdle! Don't dawdle!" he called to them.

More interested in pixies and elves than plants and leaves, Barty ambled along peering into shadows hoping to find something magic. It wasn't long before the other animals had disappeared out of sight.

While Barty was wondering whether to go on or to go back, a funny noise reached his ears. "Ooh! Ouch! Grr! Yow!" it went. He thought it might be one of his classmates in trouble so he hurried off to help. But it wasn't a bunny or a squirrel that he found tangled up in a bramble bush making a terrible fuss, it was Edwin. When the elf spotted Barty he yelled, "don't just stand there with your mouth open, you stupid bunny, help me out!"

But Barty wasn't feeling very friendly towards the elf, not after that episode with the acorn, and instead of lending a paw he simply said, "why should I?"

Edwin was astonished. He thought the bunny would do anything he asked. "Er... er... because I helped you find your way home the other day when you were lost."

"No you didn't," argued Barty, "my sister said she laid the trail of bluebells that led me through the forest."

"And who do you think made her put those bluebells there?" Edwin retorted. "I told you, magic isn't all flashes of light and disappearing in a puff of smoke."

Barty looked confused and Edwin could tell that he was winning him over, but then he got a bit too clever for his own good.

"And what about this morning, I gave you a good laugh when I hit that old Professor with the acorn, didn't I?"

"That wasn't funny. I nearly got into trouble for that," said Barty. "You know I think I'd be better off leaving you exactly where you are," and he started hopping away.

Edwin looked worried. He was covered in scratches, his clothes were in tatters and every time he struggled the

brambles held him more tightly. The only way out of that bush was with Barty's help and he would somehow have to coax the bunny back.

"Oh Barty, please come back," he said in a pleading sort of voice. But Barty took no notice.

"If you help me I'll ...I'll make your wish come true ..."

That did it, Barty was back in a trice. "Will you promise to be my friend and not get me into any more trouble?"

"An intelligent elf like *me* friends with a stupid bunny, why, it's out of the question. Whatever would fairy folk say?" said the indignant elf, but then he saw Barty hop away again. "All right, I'll be your friend," he sighed.

"Promise?" insisted Barty.

"Promise. Now get me out of here at once!"

As soon as he was out of the bramble bush, Edwin became his old self again.

"Well, must be off. Got to get a new suit of clothes."

"You won't forget your promise, will you?" asked Barty, anxiously.

"What promise was that?" teased Edwin.

"To be my friend and not to get me into trouble," reminded Barty.

"No, Barty Bob-a-Long, I won't forget. Unfortunately we elves are forbidden to break a promise," he said seriously. Then a wicked grin lit up his face. "But if you should happen to get yourself into a spot of trouble that wouldn't be my fault, would it?" And with that he was gone.

Whether he disappeared or ran off Barty couldn't tell, but he could tell that someone was standing behind him. It was Professor Bounder who had been looking everywhere for him and was not at all pleased.

"You know, Barty, your first day at school has not been a great success," his teacher said as they made their way back to Oak Tree School. "I hope that tomorrow you will do a little better."

"Oh yes," thought Barty. "Tomorrow will be better. With an elf for a friend who knows what I'll be able to do."

The BOB~A~LONG BUNNIES
← THE BALLET CLASS →

It was spring when the Bob-a-Long bunnies first moved to the old oak tree in the middle of the forest. Now it was summer and warm enough for the twins, Buffy and Bonnie, to be left outside on a blanket of leaves while Mrs. Bob-a-Long swept and tidied and Mr. Bob-a-Long went foraging for food.

Blossom and Barty had been attending
Professor Bounder's Oak Tree School all this time and
Blossom was doing very well indeed. Barty spent too
much time dreaming to be good at lessons and he
wasn't much better at sport either. He was clumsy at
jumping and butter-paws at catching and none of the
other bunnies ever wanted him on their team.

Poor Barty, nothing seemed to go right for him. He hadn't seen Edwin the elf since the day he rescued him from the brambles. At first, Barty had felt hurt, then cross, then he forgot about feeling cross and started taking long strolls in the forest in the hope of seeing Edwin again. He would often return with strange stones and twigs, which he hoped might have magic powers, and he would let his young brother and sister play with them before putting them on the shelf in his burrow.

One afternoon after school, when Barty was on one of his strolls, Blossom came rushing home all excited. Her best friend, Flora Furrypaws, was going to have ballet lessons and please could she have them too? Her parents happily agreed and Blossom rushed off to tell Flora the good news.

After she'd gone, Mrs. Bob-a-Long became quiet and thoughtful. Finally she spoke. "You know dear, it might be a good idea for Barty to have ballet lessons. Perhaps they'd cure him of his clumsiness."

"We'll have to do something about it. He fell over the twins three times yesterday and Professor Bounder says he's so bad at sport no one will have him on their team."

Mr. Bob-a-Long sat up. "Well in that case," he said, "we'd better give it a try!"

Barty arrived home carrying a knobbly piece of root which he dangled over the heads of Buffy and Bonnie. Bits of earth dropped into their cot and Mrs. Bob-a-Long made him take it outside.

"Really, Barty.
What you want with all
those sticks and stones
you keep in your room I
honestly don't know. It
takes me all morning to
dust them. I've half a
mind to make you throw
them out as well."

The thought of his mother throwing out his magic collection made Barty feel quite gloomy and the next piece of news did nothing to cheer him. Mr. and Mrs. Bob-a-Long told him that he was to have ballet lessons along with his sister.

Ballet was taught by Madame Choufleur, a very unusual bunny who wore a shawl flung over one shoulder, a flower tucked behind an ear and spoke in a different way to all the other bunnies.

"Come now, my leetle bunnykins," she would say, "hold ze paws up in ze air. Take leetle hops not beeg ones, zen you will not trip over ze feet."

Blossom and Barty sulked all the way to their first ballet class. Barty was sulking because he didn't want to learn to dance and Blossom because she didn't want her brother there to show her up.

from a wood mouse who played ballet music on a little reed pipe, Barty was the only boy there and he felt really foolish standing with a lot of giggling girl bunnies.

"Quiet please, bunnykins," ordered Madame, "ze class she has begun. Ready now, one two, three ...."

Barty was surprisingly good at ballet. He hopped and leaped and twirled without falling over once. It was something to do with the music and the way that Madame Choufleur counted each step that told him exactly where to put his feet and when. Madame was delighted with her pupil.

"I shall devise a new ballet especially for the summer concert and Barty will be ze star. He will play a prince and Blossom ze princess."

"Try not to fall down too many times," she whispered as Madame Choufleur welcomed them to her class. Apart

Barty wasn't sure how he felt about starring in a ballet. It was nice to be good at something, but everyone came to the oak tree summer concert including all his classmates and they'd be bound to laugh at him afterwards. Barty decided to take a stroll in the forest to think things out.

When he was among the trees with no one to see him, Barty couldn't resist trying out a few ballet steps. He chose to perform a rather difficult triple turn with a backwards leap, but without the music or Madame's counting, his feet tied themselves together and he flopped to the ground. Squeals of laughter

came from behind a tree where a squirrel and two
bunnies had been watching. The squirrel started to
make fun of him and to call him names like Barty
Fall-About and Barty Trip-a-Lot. Then he began
pushing Barty to see if he would fall over and the
bunnies joined in.

Just when Barty was about to burst into tears,
the branches of a nearby tree shook as though being
blown by a strong breeze and tiny crab apples fell
onto the heads of the squirrel and two bunnies. They
didn't hurt them, but they frightened them away.
Barty was about to go too when who should drop
right into his path, but Edwin the elf.

"Got rid of those chaps pretty quick, didn't I?" he bragged. "What in Elfdom were you trying to do just then, tie yourself in knots?" Barty told Edwin all about ballet lessons and about how he was going to star in the summer concert.

"Concert? I like a concert. I might even come along to see that. Should be good for a laugh, anyway. Well I must be off. Ta ta."

"Wait," screamed Barty. "You promised you would be my friend and yet you haven't been to see me for ages."

"Of course I'm your friend," said the elf. "I 'magicked' you out of a spot of trouble just then, didn't I?"

"That wasn't magic," grumbled Barty, "you happened to be in that tree so you shook the branches and made the apples fall."

"Being in the right place at the right time is magic," corrected Edwin. "And it's time that I wasn't here." Once again the elf went away without Barty seeing how.

The concert was taking place on the grass in front of a semi-circle of trees. At either side of the 'stage' was a clump of bushes from which the performers could enter and exit. Most of the animals who lived around the oak tree were there watching, but none so proud as Mr. and Mrs. Bob-a-Long. They had even brought Buffy and Bonnie along to see their brother and sister dance.

The ballet was the last item on the programme and when the wood mouse struck up a tune on his pipe, 'Princess' Blossom and her attendants danced onto the stage. They looked so pretty wearing coronets of flowers on their heads and garlands around their waists. Out of sight of the audience, 'Prince' Barty was waiting to make his entrance. He

was wearing a coronet of leaves and held a stick that was made to look like a sword. Hearing the music stop suddenly, Barty parted the bushes to see what was wrong. A nasty looking stoat had somehow got onto the stage and had all the dancers huddled together in a corner, trembling with fear.

Usually the older bunnies would keep a look out for danger and if they sensed trouble coming they would warn the others to get back in

their burrows for safety. But today, with everyone at the concert, the stoat had managed to creep through the forest unnoticed and was now smacking his lips as he decided which of the bunnies to carry off. No one dared move.

Barty desperately tried to think what to do, but he was not a naturally brave bunny and anyway he was rooted to the spot. A tap on the shoulder set him shaking like a leaf, certain that another stoat was after him.

"Touch of stage fright, eh, Barty?" said Edwin, who had appeared from nowhere. "Don't worry. Once you're out there in front of an audience the butterflies just disappear. You'll see." And before Barty could tell him about the stoat, the elf had pushed him onto the stage with such force that his coronet fell over his eyes.

Barty couldn't see a thing. He blindly stumbled about the stage trying to get off, but his feet seemed to be going one way and his body another and he lunged forward in an effort to stop himself from falling. He was still holding the swordstick and its point stuck right into the tip of the stoat's tail, pinning it to the ground. The animal let out a shriek, whipped round and tugged his tail free. The sword snapped and Barty fell back. Clutching his tail and whimpering, the stoat fled from the stage into the forest.

There was a cheer from the audience and when Barty lifted the coronet from his eyes, all the little bunnies were gathered around thanking him for saving them and telling him how brave he had been.

Barty was the hero of the day. That night, the oak tree animals gave a big party in his honour. There was plenty to eat and drink and music for dancing. Barty finally got to perform his part in the ballet and nobody laughed, not even the two bunnies and the squirrel who had called him names. Now they wanted to be his friend.

Only one thing would have made it better
and that was if his friend Edwin could have been
there. He thought, once or twice, that he saw the elf
sitting in a tree grinning at him, but it was
dark and Barty was feeling much
too sleepy to be sure.

The BOB~A~LONG BUNNIES
A DAY AT THE FAIR

Mr. Bob-a-Long looked up from his newspaper and beamed at his family as though he had some surprise in store for them. He had. "How would you all like to go to the fair? There's one today in Buttercup Meadow. We could take a picnic too."

"Hurray," shouted Blossom. "I love fairs and picnics."

The twins, Buffy and Bonnie, cheered
too, although they weren't quite sure what they
were cheering for.

Barty kept quiet. He wasn't keen on
fairs. The last time he went to one he climbed
to the top of the helter-skelter and felt too dizzy
to slide down. His father had had to rescue
him.

"A picnic's very nice," began Mrs Bob-a-
Long, "but it's a lot of work as well."

"Don't worry, dear," said her husband,
"we'll all help. Barty you go and find the picnic
hamper while Blossom clears away the
breakfast things."

"Can I ask Flora to come with us?" asked Blossom, as she picked up the bowls and spoons. "Then I'll have someone to go on the rides with." Flora Furrypaws was her best friend.

Her mother frowned. "What about your brother? Can't you go on the rides with him?"

"Oh, no!" exclaimed Blossom. "He's no fun. He gets dizzy just looking at the helter-skelter. I want someone who doesn't get scared."

Barty, who had found the picnic hamper, was hovering in the doorway. Blossom saw him and her whiskers twitched as she realised he had heard every word she'd said.

Flora arrived wearing a pretty straw hat
trimmed with flowers which made Blossom
rush off and put on her best ribbons.

Soon everyone was ready. The twins
were put into one half of a hollowed out log
and the hamper was loaded onto the other.

"Shall I pull the hamper?" offered Barty.

"Er. . .better not," grinned his father.
"You nearly lost all the furniture when we
moved to the old oak tree. I certainly don't
want you losing our lunch."

The sun was crackling through the
branches of the trees and Barty soon felt

drowsy. He was looking forward to eating the picnic and finding a quiet spot where he could dream that he was brave enough to climb the highest peak in bunnydom without getting dizzy.

Leaving the forest behind, the Bob-a-Longs came to a grassy bank covered in buttercups.

"This looks like a good spot for a picnic," declared Mr. Bob-a-Long, "let's stop here."

Blossom spread out a blanket for Bonnie and Buffy to play on and Mrs Bob-a-Long spread out a tablecloth for the food. And what a mouth-watering sight it was.

After they had eaten, Barty felt very full and rather sleepy. He lay back on the grass and closed his eyes. It seemed like a perfect day.

"No sign of a fair. Perhaps it's gone away," he thought hopefully.

Then he heard music. At first he thought he was dreaming, but when he opened his eyes he could still hear it. So could Blossom, who was scrambling up the bank in the direction of the sound with Flora close behind.

"It's the fair! It's the fair!" she yelled, jumping up and down with glee. "There's the big wheel and roundabouts and a helter-skelter. Oh, come on, Flora, I want to go on everything." And the two of them rushed down the bank into the noisy crowd.

Carrying a twin each and with Barty tagged on, Mr. and Mrs Bob-a-Long watched the girls go up and down, round and round and even upside down. They shrieked with laughter and didn't seem afraid of anything. Barty felt a little envious.

"Why don't you take the twins on the swing-boats," suggested his mother. "They look nice and gentle."

Barty reluctantly agreed and the twins were put on one seat while he sat facing them on the other.

It was a gentle ride. To and fro it went. To and fro. Buffy and Bonnie loved it and pulled on their rope to go higher. That was too much for Barty. His ears started to droop and his eyes went around and around. Mr. Bob-a-Long had to stop the swing-boat and help him out.

"Blossom's right," thought Barty, "I'm not much fun."

Feeling rather gloomy, and a bit dizzy, he wandered round alone until he came to a gaily striped tent with a sign saying - FORTUNE TELLER - I SEE THE FUTURE.

"Why don't you come in," said a voice.

"Well I can't get dizzy on this," muttered the bunny, as in he went.

It was dark inside, but he could make out someone sitting at a table on which there was a glass ball. The figure was dressed from head to toe in long robes.

"Sit down," the voice commanded and Barty did as he was told.

"So, Barty Bob-a-Long, you wish to know what the future holds."

Barty nearly fell off his seat. "Y. . .y. . .you know my name," he gasped.

"Gypsy Edwina knows everything. Cross my palm with silver and I'll tell your fortune."

"I haven't got any silver," Barty told her.

"Then what have you got? I don't tell fortunes for nothing," she snapped.

Barty felt in his pocket and pulled out a piece of carrot pie which he'd been saving.

"That'll do," said the gypsy, snatching it greedily. "Now, gaze into my crystal ball."

Barty gazed and gazed, but could see nothing.

"Aah!" cried Gypsy Edwina. "The mists are clearing. I see a bright future for you, young Bob-a-Long. You will be going up in the

world. You will reach heights you never thought possible." Her voice was growing shrill and she was waving her arms wildly. "You will rise ever upwards and nothing will stop you," she screeched. "Nothing!" Then, "next, please," she called in a very down to earth voice.

"Is that all?" complained Barty.

"Have you any more pie?"

"Er. . .no," he replied.

"Then that's all. Goodbye."

Barty left feeling more than a little put out. "Anyone could have said what she said," he grumbled to himself. It certainly wasn't worth a slice of his mother's best carrot pie.

The sight of his mother and father hurrying towards him pushed Gypsy Edwina to the back of his mind for the time being. Mrs Bob-a-Long was crying and Mr. Bob-a-Long looked most concerned.

"Oh, Barty, something dreadful has happened," sobbed his mother. "Blossom and Flora are stuck at the top of the big wheel."

Flora's straw hat had blown off and got caught up in the machinery that turned the wheel. It had ground to a halt, leaving the girls perched periously at the top. Flora was standing up and screaming which made their seat rock violently.

"Do sit down," begged Blossom. "Can't you see that you're making things worse."

"Why doesn't somebody do something?" cried poor Mrs Bob-a-Long.

The bunny who worked the ride had tried to climb up and release the hat, but he was too heavy and had made the whole thing shake; which had started Flora screaming.

"What we need is someone who can climb up and free that hat," he announced. "Someone who is small and who doesn't mind the heights."

A strange feeling came over Barty. Hadn't the gypsy said something about 'going up in the world' and 'reaching new heights'? Perhaps this was what she was talking about. He started to feel quite excited. "Perhaps I'm meant to rescue Blossom and Flora." And

without thinking, Barty pushed through the crowd and began to climb up through the big wheel.

"What does Barty think he's doing?" gasped Mrs Bob-a-Long.

"I think he's trying to free Flora's hat," said her husband proudly.

"Has he forgotten that heights make him dizzy," she wailed.

"Oh, dear," Mr. Bob-a-Long muttered. "I think he must have."

Barty was only a paw's length away
from the hat when he remembered that heights
make him dizzy. He looked down at the crowd
and it swam before his eyes; so he shut them.
Then he started to lose his grip. The crowd
held its breath.

"Come on, Barty, come on," urged
Blossom. "You're almost there."

But he couldn't move. He was too
scared even to open his eyes. "I can't do it. I'm
going to fall."

Then Gypsy Edwina's words came to
him as though she was whispering them in his

ear. 'You will rise ever upward and nothing will stop you.' Barty's courage returned. The gypsy had seen all this in her crystal ball and nothing would stop him. He wasn't going to fall. He would be all right.

He opened his eyes and with one supreme effort he stretched out, grasped the hat and tossed it into the crowd. The machinery started to move and Blossom's and Flora's chair slowly descended with Barty hanging from it. Everyone cheered. Mr. and Mrs Bob-a-Long heaved a heavy sigh of relief.

Blossom rushed up and flung her arms
around her brother. "Thank you, Barty. Thank
you for saving us. You were so brave." Then
she looked a little embarrassed. "I'm sorry I
said you weren't any fun. I'm proud that you're
my brother."

Flora tried to thank him but had lost her
voice from screaming.

"I think it's time we were getting home,"
said Mr. Bob-a-Long. "We've had enough
excitement for one day."

As they were leaving the fairground,
Barty spotted a gypsy figure slipping out

through the back of the tent. "Won't be long," he told the others as he dashed after her.

To his great surprise Edwina started to throw off her gypsy robes to reveal underneath the familiar tunic of an elf.

"Edwin!" cried Barty.

Edwin turned, his mouth was crammed full with carrot pie. "Oh, hello, Bob-a-Long. Pretty good stunt you pulled up there. I was impressed. Didn't know you had it in you."

Barty felt uneasy. "B. . .but you knew I was going to do it. You told me so. You saw it in your crystal ball."

Edwin threw back his head and laughed. "That? Oh, that was just a lot of nonsense that I made up. You came into the tent looking so sorry for yourself that I thought I'd tell you something that would cheer you up. Give you confidence, a bit of get up and go. Worked, didn't it?"

Barty's ears were beginning to droop. "You mean I could have fallen?"

"Quite possible," grinned the elf, "but you didn't."

Barty didn't hear his last words for he had fainted clean away.

When the Bob-a-Longs came back to find their son he was propped up against a tent. He was looking and feeling most peculiar and although his feet were firmly on the ground, he was as dizzy as if he was perched on the very top of the big wheel.

The
BOB~A~LONG BUNNIES
◄— ◆ —► BARTY'S BIG ADVENTURE ◄— ◆ —►

"Come along now, which one of you
bunnies is going to be the first to walk the
plank?" said One-Eyed Wally, the pirate chief,
rubbing his hands with glee. Having captured
the good ship *Bobalina* and its cargo of carrots
he was looking forward to sending its crew to
the bottom of the sea.

Horatio Hop-a-Lot, captain of the *Bobalina*, was about to step onto the plank when up jumped the cabin boy. "I will. I will. I'll be the first!" he cried.

"Blistering barnacles!" exclaimed Wally. "You're a bold un, and no mistake. Makes no difference to me which one of you goes first so long as them sharks gets their dinner," and he laughed cruelly and prodded the young bunny with his cutlass.

Barty Bob-a-Long hopped onto the plank and, smiling bravely at his shipmates, shuffled along to the end. Instead of stepping off into the swirling sea, he started to bounce up and down, getting higher and higher. The pirates got dizzy watching him. "Stop that," yelled Wally. "You're making me feel seasick."

"Sorry," grinned Barty. With one big bounce he flew into the air, performed three perfect backward somersaults and landed on the pirates, squashing the breath out of them. Before they could recover, Barty had removed their weapons and tied them up.

"Well done, lad," said Captain Hop-a-Lot. "I shall see that you are rewarded for your courage and daring. But first we must deliver our cargo of carrots. Take the wheel *Mr. Bob-a-Long*, and set a course for home."

"Aye-aye, captain," said the proud bunny.

"What did you say?" asked Professor Bounder.

Barty sat blinking as the *Bobalina* and its crew disappeared and the familiar faces of his classmates came into view. He was back on dry land.

"What did you say?" repeated his teacher.

"Please, sir, he said aye-aye'," giggled a helpful mouse. Barty scowled at it.

"Yes, that's what I thought he said," murmured the bemused Bounder. "Now I want you to stand up and tell me what you have learnt today about the Great Carrot Famine - one of the most important events in bunny history."

One by one the class stood up and said their piece. When it was Barty's turn he stood up and opened his mouth, but nothing came out. He hadn't heard a word of the lesson.

The professor tapped his stick impatiently. "I am waiting for you to tell me what you have learned, Bob-a-Long. And what is more, no-one will go home until you do!"

The whole class glared at Barty. "Say something," hissed a squirrel, "we don't want to be here all day."

The only thing Barty could think of was to tell him about his dream. There were carrots in that somewhere. It might even have had something to do with the lesson, he thought hopefully. He gulped, took a deep breath and began. "There was this ship bringing barrels of carrots to the starving bunnies but it was seized by some wicked pirates who were going to throw the barrels overboard and make the

crew walk the plank." He paused and looked
around. Everyone seemed quite interested. He
took courage and went on.

"But then I . . . I mean this cabin boy
captured the pirates single-handed, the
captain made him first mate and he brought
home the carrots to all the hungry bunnies."
Barty sat down, rather pleased with himself.

Professor Bounder looked as if he was about to burst. "What nonsense," he spluttered. "It is obvious that you haven't listened to a word I've said. In fact, you never listen. You spend all your time dreaming. It's time I had a serious talk with your parents. I shall visit them this very afternoon." And off he went in a dreadful mood.

Everyone began to drift off home. Blossom was so ashamed of her brother that she rushed away without waiting for him. But Barty didn't care. He was glad. He wasn't going home anyway. He had decided to run away.

In his head a plan was taking shape. He would follow the brook that burbled along past the old oak tree until it joined the river. Then he would follow the course of the river until it flowed into the sea. After that he would stow away on a big ship that sailed the world and he would capture pirates and meet mermaids and no-one would know that he'd been such a dunce at school. He hurried on, eager to start his big adventure.

Passing a clump of reeds, he noticed a
flash of bright colour and, curious to see what
it was, he pushed them aside to look. He
expected to see a bird or a flower but found
himself gazing on the trimmest toy boat that
ever set sail. It was as though it had been
waiting to carry him off on his big adventure
and Barty wasted no time in scrambling
aboard. He pushed against the bank to float
downstream. "This is the way to travel," he
sighed.

It was a glorious afternoon. The warmth of the sun and the gentle bobbing of the boat sent Barty drifting off to dreamland where he danced with mermaids in King Neptune's palace. Some birds twittered with laughter as Barty sailed by. It was rather a small boat and Barty was rather a tubby bunny.

A big drop of rain woke him up. Plop! Then another and another. The sky was full of dark clouds and the little boat was caught up in some reeds. The rain came faster, filling the boat until it began to sink. Luckily for Barty the stream was quite shallow and he was able to scramble ashore. Soaked to the skin and feeling very sorry for himself, he followed the stream back towards the old oak tree, back towards home.

The boat hadn't actually carried him
very far and it wasn't long before he saw the
tree's friendly branches. Barty felt as though
he'd been a million miles away from home and
although he knew he was going to be in
trouble he was glad to see the warm glow from
the entrance to his burrow.

"Barty, wherever have you been? You're
soaking wet. Why didn't you come home when
it started to rain?" his mother scolded.

"Professor Bounder here has been waiting for you," she continued. "Tells me he has something to say."

The professor stood up and coughed. He looked dreadfully serious.

"Uh-oh, here it comes. I'm in trouble now," thought Barty.

"Er . . .young Barty," the professor began, "I believe that I owe you an apology."

Barty couldn't believe his ears.

"It appears that your story about a ship bringing a cargo of carrots to save the starving bunnies was true. It says here." He opened up the book he was holding, which was large and dusty and its pages were yellow with age. "Why the other history books don't mention it I'm sure I don't know. For once you seem to know more than your teacher." He smiled and patted Barty on the head.

Professor Bounder stayed for tea and never mentioned how cross he had been with Barty that morning.

Mrs. Bob-a-Long was showing him out when he suddenly stopped and held a paw up in the air. "I almost forgot . . ." he began. Barty tried to hide under the table. "That bit about the pirates was in the book, too." He riffled through the pages. "It says that a young cabin boy thwarted their plans and saved the cargo. Bunny by the name of Bob-a-Long. Isn't that odd. An ancestor of yours, perhaps?"

The next day, Professor Bounder made
Barty tell the story all over again so that the
class could copy it into their history books. He
enjoyed telling it this time and made the
pirates more wicked and the brave bunny
more daring. Everyone clapped when he'd
finished.

Walking back to his desk he saw
something glinting in the trees. It was probably
the sun playing on the leaves; although it
might have been a certain elf grinning at him
and it occurred to Barty that maybe Edwin had
had a hand in all this. But then he thought, no,
not even Edwin would dare to re-write bunny
history - or would he?